Disney

This magical book belongs to:

Sierra

Chiara Too

Disney's
Magical World
of Reading

① Bambi   **②** Dumbo

Adapted by Kathryn Knight
Art Direction by Andy Mangrum

14793-1105 Magical World of Reading - Bambi and Dumbo
06 07 08 09 CCO 10 9 8 7 6 5 4 3 2 1

Walt Disney's
Bambi

*This is the story of a fawn who grew up
to be the Great Prince of the Forest.*

Deep in the forest,

on a nice Spring morning,

a prince was born.

It was a baby deer—a fawn.

His name was Bambi.

Animals and birds came to see the new prince.

When Bambi woke up
he saw happy faces all around him.
A friendly rabbit said,
"My name is Thumper."
Bambi smiled.

Bambi went with his mother to see the forest.

They met Mother Quail and her nine babies.

"Good morning, young Prince," they called.

Bambi liked the forest.

He liked all the friendly animals.

One day, Bambi and Thumper were playing.

Birds sang and flew over their heads.

Thumper pointed at one.

"That's a bird," he said.

Bambi called out, "Bird!"

Then a butterfly fluttered by.

Bambi called out, "Bird!"

"No," giggled Thumper, "that's a butterfly."

Bambi turned to a pretty flower.

"Butterfly!" he shouted.

Thumper laughed.

"No," he cried, "that's a flower!"

Then, Bambi bent down to smell the flowers.

Suddenly, a head popped up!

A small black and white head.

"Flower!" said Bambi again.

Thumper laughed and laughed.

"That's not a flower, that's a skunk!"
said Thumper.

The little skunk looked at Bambi.

"That's all right," the skunk said.

"He can call me Flower if he wants to."

And Bambi and Thumper and Flower
all became good friends.

Bambi's mother took him to a new place.

It was the wide, open meadow.

Bambi met another fawn.

Her name was Faline.

She smiled at Bambi.

Bambi and Faline became friends, too.

Just then, Bambi saw a tall stag.

It was the Great Prince of the Forest.

The Great Prince was Bambi's father.

He came to tell the other deer to run.

There was danger nearby!

Run! Run!

Bambi ran to the trees.

He was afraid.

But his father led him to his mother.

"Man was in the forest," she said.

Summer passed.

Fall passed.

Soon it was very cold.

One morning, everything was white!

Bambi's mother said, "That is snow.

Winter has come."

Bambi jumped into the snow.

Plop!

Bambi found Thumper.

Thumper was sliding on the ice.

"Come on, Bambi," called Thumper.

"You can slide too!"

Bambi ran over to Thumper.

But Bambi's feet were too small!

He could not slide around on the ice.

He fell down onto his tummy.

Thud!

Thumper showed Bambi how to

stand on the ice.

Then Bambi could slide, too.

Winter was fun.

But soon there was less and less food.

Bambi and his mother had to eat

the bark from the trees.

One day, Bambi and his mother
went to the meadow to look for food.
They found a little bit of green grass
peeping out of the snow.
Bambi and his mother ate the grass.
Suddenly, Bambi's mother looked up.
She sniffed the air.
Danger!
"Go back to the forest!" she told Bambi.
"Quickly! Run!"

Bambi ran and ran.

"Run faster," said his mother.

There was a loud—*bang!*

Bambi ran all the way to the forest.

But where was his mother?

"Mother! Where are you?" he cried.

There was no answer.

Then Bambi saw his father.
"Your mother cannot be with you
any longer," he told Bambi.
And Bambi's father walked him home.

Winter passed.

Spring came to the forest.

Bambi grew to be a fine young stag.

One day, Friend Owl looked at the birds.

They were snuggling and twittering.

"They are twitterpated!" said Friend Owl
to Bambi, Thumper, and Flower.

"It happens every spring!"

"It won't happen to me!" Bambi said.

"Me neither," Thumper agreed.

Just then, a pretty girl rabbit hopped over.

Thumper left to play with the new rabbit.

"Twitterpated!" said Bambi.

Bambi stopped to drink at a small pond.

A voice said, "Hello, Bambi."

It was Faline!

Faline leaned over and licked Bambi's face.

And he became twitterpated too!

Bambi and Faline were happy together.

Spring passed.

And summer passed.

One fall morning, Bambi smelled the air.

He smelled smoke!

He went to the top of a cliff.

His father was there, too.

"Man is in the forest," said his father.

"See the campfires? We must go deep
into the forest—quickly!"

27

Bambi ran to find Faline.

She was trapped!

A pack of hunting dogs snapped at her.

Bambi rushed at the dogs.

Faline jumped and ran to the river.

Bambi turned to follow Faline.

Suddenly—*bang!*

Bambi felt pain in his shoulder.

He fell to the ground.

"Get up, Bambi!" a voice cried.

"We must go to the lake.

The forest is on fire.

Follow me!"

Bambi opened his eyes.

His father was beside him.

Bambi slowly stood up.

He followed his father.

They came to a big waterfall.

They jumped!

Down and down they fell
to the water below.

They waded to an island.

Faline and the animals were there.

The fire burned and burned.

But then the fire burned out.

The animals went back to the forest.

When spring came,

new grass and flowers grew.

The forest was beautiful once again.

One morning, Friend Owl
told the good news.
Bambi and Faline had a family.
All the animals and birds
came to see Faline
and her two new fawns

Standing nearby was the proud father.

It was Bambi, the new

Great Prince of the Forest.

WALT DISNEP'S
DUMBO

This is the story of a little elephant
with a big heart, and two very big ears,
who learned to soar.

Look up in the sky!
Storks are flying above
the circus train.
Storks are bringing baby animals
to the mother animals.

Mrs. Jumbo said,

"I hope there is a baby for me."

A stork flew to Mrs. Jumbo.
He had a large bundle.
It was a baby elephant!
"I'll call him
Jumbo Junior,"
said Mrs. Jumbo.

The other elephants looked at the baby.
"Look at him!" they said. "Isn't he cute?"

Just then, the baby elephant sneezed.

Ah-choo!

Oh, my! Two big ears flapped out.

The other elephants giggled.

"He looks funny," said one elephant.

"Let's call him Dumbo."

Mrs. Jumbo loved her baby—
big ears and all!
She lifted him up in her trunk
and rocked him to sleep.

The next day was the circus parade!
The band played.

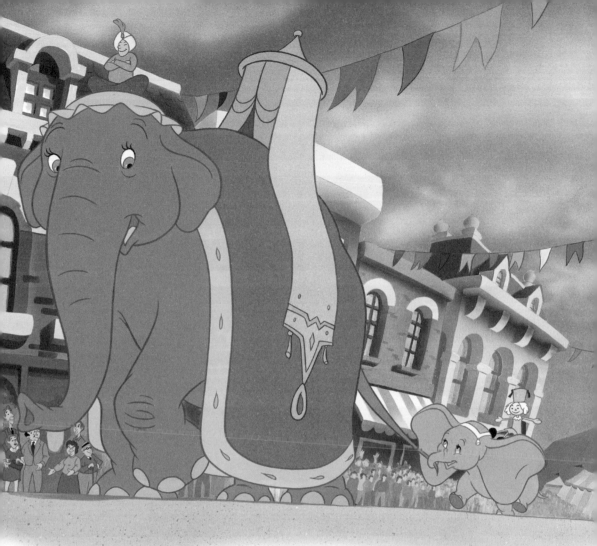

The clowns and animals
marched down the street.
And people clapped and cheered.

Children went to the big circus tent.

They went to see the animals.

One boy pointed at Dumbo.

"Look at his ears!" he said.

The boys made fun of Dumbo.

Then one of them pulled
the little elephant's ears!
This made Mrs. Jumbo very angry!
Very, very angry!
The boys screamed and ran away.

Soon, Dumbo's mother was taken away.
She was locked in a small cage
far away from Dumbo.

Poor Dumbo.

He was sad without his mother.

The other elephants did not speak to him.

He was all alone.

A mouse called Timothy saw Dumbo.

He felt sorry for the little elephant.

"I'll be your friend,"

Timothy told Dumbo.

"In fact, I'll bet we can make you a star.

All we need is a good plan...."

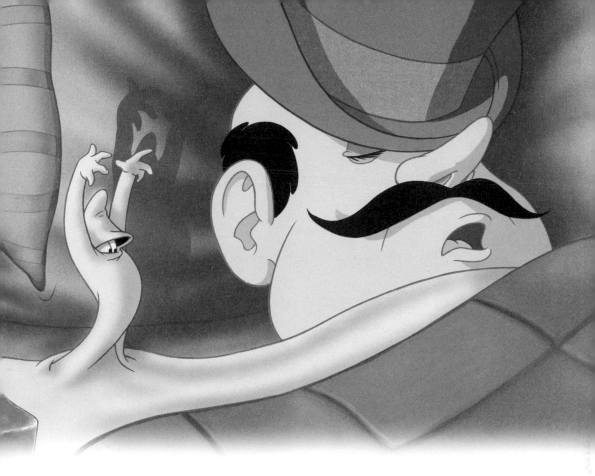

As soon as the Ringmaster was asleep,
Timothy went into his tent.
He scampered up to the
Ringmaster's ear and said,
"You should put the little elephant in the show.
The little elephant with the big ears. Dumbo!"
"Dumbo…" mumbled the Ringmaster.
"Dumbo…"

The Ringmaster did put Dumbo
in the show.
But, oh, no!
When Dumbo ran to jump
onto the top elephant, he tripped!
He tripped over his big ears.
He bumped into the elephants,
and down they came.
Bump, bump, bump!

Next, the Ringmaster made Dumbo
into a clown.
He dressed Dumbo like a baby.
He had to jump down onto a hoop.
Dumbo was afraid to jump—but he did!
Down, down, down he went…

...and under that hoop was a tub of goo!
Everyone laughed when Dumbo
landed in the goo.
But Dumbo was not happy at all.

"We will go see your mother!"
said Timothy.
This made Dumbo happy.
Mrs. Jumbo put out her trunk.
She cuddled Dumbo and sang to him.
But then it was time for Dumbo to go.
Sadly, he fell asleep,
and dreamed and dreamed....

The next morning,

Dumbo was not in the tent.

He was up in a tree!

"Look at that elephant in the tree!"

said a crow.

"How did he get up there?"

Dumbo woke up.

He tried to grab the branch
with his trunk, but it snapped.
Dumbo and Timothy tumbled down
into a pond.
"How did we get in that tree?"
said Timothy.

"Maybe you flew!" joked one of the crows.

"Yes, that's it!" cried Timothy.

"You flew up there, Dumbo!"

The little elephant looked surprised.

He couldn't really fly—could he?

Timothy said, "You just have to believe

in yourself, Dumbo."

One crow gave Timothy a feather.

"This is a magic feather," the crow said.

"It will help Dumbo fly!"

Dumbo held the feather in his trunk.

He stood at the edge of a cliff...

...and off he went!

All at once, Dumbo was flapping his ears.

He was flying in the air!

"You did it!" cried Timothy.

That night at the circus,
Dumbo was not afraid.
He had his magic feather.
He knew he could fly.

Timothy was tucked inside Dumbo's hat.

"Okay," he said. "Take off!"

Just as the little elephant leaped into the air,

he dropped the feather!

Dumbo began to fall!

Timothy cried, "Flap your ears!

You can fly! You can!"

Dumbo began to flap his ears
as fast as he could.
Suddenly, Dumbo was flying!
He did not need that feather after all!
Wow! Everyone cheered!
Dumbo was a star!

The Ringmaster was very happy.
He let Mrs. Jumbo out of the cage.
Now she could ride
in a nice car on the train.
She was very happy.

And Dumbo was very, very happy!